To Patrick, Conor and Colleen, with big, big love.
—J.G.

To Cindy, for her love and encouragement
and to Murphy, for being my Marley.
—R.C.

First published in hardback in the USA by HarperCollins Publishers Inc. in 2007
First published in paperback in Great Britain by HarperCollins Children's Books in 2007

1 3 5 7 9 10 8 6 4 2

ISBN-10: 0-00-725478-4
ISBN-13: 978-0-00-725478-1

HarperCollins Children's Books is a division of HarperCollins Publishers Ltd.

Text and illustrations copyright © John Grogan 2007

Typography by Jeanne L. Hogle

Visit our website at: www.harpercollinschildrensbooks.co.uk

Colour Reproduction by Dot Gradations Ltd, UK
Printed and bound by Rotolito Lombarda, Italy

John Grogan

Bad Dog, Marley!

Illustrated by Richard Cowdrey

HarperCollins *Children's Books*

In a little house on Churchill Road lived a very happy family.

There was one mummy, one daddy, one freckle-faced girl named Cassie and one crawly, squirmy boy named Baby Louie. He had a giant, droopy nappy and a thumb that rarely left his mouth.

The family had two budgies, three goldfish and four pet crickets. But there was one thing the family did not have, and that was a dog.

"Oh, please, please, please, please," begged Cassie. "Please, can we get a puppy?"

"Peas!" cried Baby Louie.

"We'll see," said Daddy.

"We'll see," said Mummy.

Cassie and Louie waited and waited until...

Daddy came home from work one day carrying a cardboard box.

"Hey, everyone! Come and see!" he yelled.

In the box was a squiggly, yellow fur ball with a wet, black nose and ears so big and floppy, they looked like he'd borrowed them from an elephant.

"A puppy!" Cassie squealed.
"Bow-wow!" cried Baby Louie.
"This," Daddy said, "is Marley."
"Ahhh," said Mummy. "Look how tiny he is."
But Marley didn't stay tiny for long.

That puppy ate and he ate and he ate. He ate what was in his dish. He ate what wasn't.

He drank and he drank and he drank. He drank what was in his bowl. He drank what wasn't.

The more he ate and the more he drank, the more
he pooped and the more he weed.

And the more he grew and grew and grew.

And the bigger Marley got, the bigger
trouble he got into. Big, big, bad-boy trouble.

Marley ate the buttons off jackets and the laces off shoes.
He tipped over his water bowl and raided the rubbish.
He pulled the toilet paper off the roll and the turkey out
of the oven. He chewed Mummy's reading glasses and
swallowed Daddy's pay cheque.

"Bad dog, Marley!"
Daddy said.
 "Bad dog, Marley!"
Mummy said.

   "Bad dog, Marley!"
Cassie said.
    "Bah boo-boo, Waddy!"
Baby Louie said.

Marley tried to be a good dog, honest he did. But everything he tried ended up being bad.

He tried to make friends with the squirrels.

"Bad dog, Marley!" Mummy said.

He tried to play house with Cassie and Louie.

"Bad dog, Marley!" Cassie said.

"Bah boo-boo, Waddy!" Baby Louie said.

He tried to find a safe hiding place during thunderstorms.

"Bad dog, Marley!" Daddy said.

One day Mummy baked cookies and left them on the counter to cool. Big mistake.

The next day Mummy baked a chocolate cake and put it high on top of the refrigerator.
"You won't get this," she said.

But Marley
got it. Every
last crumb.

Another time Marley jumped over the fence and came home with a giant pair of pants.

"I don't even want to know," Daddy said.

One day Marley finally went too far.
The family came home
from a movie to find an indoor
snowstorm. There in the corner
of the living room was the
Abominable Snowmarley.
"Uh-oh," said Baby Louie.

"That's it," Mummy said. "That dog has got to GO!"

"Please, Mummy," Cassie cried. "Marley didn't mean it. He can't help it."

"I'm sorry," Mummy said. "I can't take it any more."

Marley was very, very sad. *I try so hard and I mess up everything. Everything!*

Daddy put an ad in the newspaper:

Big Yellow Dog — a little crazy but with a pure heart. Free to good home.

Strangers came to meet the big, crazy, pure-hearted dog
and every one received the same royal Marley welcome.
"No, thanks," they all said.

Then one day Marley proved he was right where he belonged.

Mummy was in the bedroom, folding clothes, when Marley started barking.

"Bad dog, Marley!" Mummy scolded. "Pipe down!"
But Marley would not pipe down. He barked and barked.

Then Mummy heard
Cassie scream, "Come quick!
It's Louie!"
   Mummy raced for the kitchen
"My baby!" she cried.

Before Mummy could take a step, Marley raced up the drawers, leaped on to the counter, jumped up on his hind legs – and grabbed Baby Louie by his great, big, droopy nappy. Marley would not let go until Mummy had her baby safe in her arms.

"Good dog, Marley!" Mummy said.

"Good dog, Marley!" Daddy said.

"Good dog, Marley!" Cassie said.

"Me go again!" Baby Louie said.

Marley jumped on the floor and did the Marley Mambo.

Finally, I did something right!

"Does this mean…?" Cassie asked.

Mummy looked at Marley doing his crazy dance. She looked at Cassie, then at Daddy. She squeezed Baby Louie in her arms. Finally she looked back at Marley.

"Oh, please, please, please, Mummy!" Cassie said.

"Peas!" Baby Louie said.

A little smile came to Mummy's face. "This is Marley's home and we are his family," she said.

"And we love him very much," Daddy added. "Slobber and all."

"So Marley can stay?" asked Cassie.

"Yes," Mummy said. "Marley can stay."

"Yay!" said Cassie.

"Yay!" said Baby Louie.

"Woof!" said Marley – and gave Mummy the biggest, fattest kiss of her life.

"Good dog, Marley!"

John Grogan's first book, *Marley & Me: Life and Love with the World's Worst Dog*, was first published in 2005 and rapidly became an international number 1 bestseller with more than 3 million copies in print and rights sold in more than two dozen languages. John is an award-winning newspaper columnist and former magazine editor. He lives with his wife and three children and their new dog, Gracie, in Pennsylvania, USA. You can visit him online at www.marleyandme.com.

Richard Cowdrey has illustrated numerous books for children. He lives in Ohio, USA, with his wife and children and their yellow Labrador, Murphy. You can visit him online at: www.rcowdrey.com.

The author *John Grogan*

© ADAM NADEL